*F*or *H*er
*D*ark *E*yes *O*nly

#2

3. 11·16

a Delta Force romance story
by
M. L. Buchman

Buchman Bookworks

Other works by M.L. Buchman

newsletter signup at:

www.mlbuchman.com

1

"Sucks!" I called out to the watch officer as I strode into the command hangar at the ass-end of Riyadh airfield. Surprising a Delta Force operator with one of my sniper-silent approaches was never a good idea. Doing it to the six-foot-two of officer who stood four inches taller than me and had much broader shoulders was an even worse one.

Part of our low profile stance in Saudi Arabia was that we ran our operation in the shadowy back corner of the most rundown hangar on the base. It was so beat-up that it captured more of the passing sandstorms than it kept out. Delta's watch post was tucked behind a small flock of Night Stalkers' helos and an Air Force four-prop C-130 cargo plane which served as our secure storage and could get us up and out in fifteen minutes if we had to jump in somewhere. At night, with only a single desk lamp on, it was a murky place of shadows and secrets.

"Kurt," was all that Lieutenant Bill Bruce grunted in reply—about as much as my greeting deserved. Two a.m. shift change, and the country was still cooking so hot that I had probably sweat out a liter just crossing over from the long banks of containerized living units—CLUs—in the US Spec Ops sector. My last leave back home on the Oregon Coast was still in my blood and the desert sucked. The six hours that Lieutenant Bruce had just spent on the watch desk also couldn't have been much of lark. So, neither of us had been issued a cheery mood.

"I swear my CLU was shipped over during Desert Storm." The container had two bunks, two chairs, and a toilet in a twenty-foot steel box with an AC unit bolted on one end that groaned, wheezed, and could sometimes drop

the inside temperature a whole ten degrees—
my home for the last six months that Delta
Force had parked my ass here.

"CLUs weren't part of inventory back
then, Sergeant." The lieutenant's ex-SEAL
was showing through. Those guys never had
a decent sense of humor, not even after
joining The Unit—what most folks call Delta
Force. We were officially CAG, the Combat
Applications Group, with a strong emphasis
on "Application."

"Maybe you could un-invent them, sir."
Then I didn't see any reason to not keep
messing with him. "I bet some supply sergeant
timewarped it back so that it would corrode
and spring sand leaks until I moved in." It
was almost plausible. I'd long since learned
to never underestimate the power of a good
quartermaster—especially if you ticked him off.

Still no response.

"I swear, thing's the same age I am and
someone should have taken it out to pasture
and shot it a long time back." I might have
done it myself if we weren't supposed to be
keeping such a low profile.

We tried to stay quiet because the Saudis

weren't big fans of having US commandos squatting in the heart of their country, no matter how badly they needed us. Being here worked for us too. From Riyadh we were four hundred klicks to Iran, Iraq, Yemen, Syria, and a dozen other disasters waiting to happen. So, during those rare pauses in between assignments, this base was where we squatted and sweat until hot metal and the almost cinnamon tang of blowing dust had become a part of who we were.

The lieutenant kept his blue-eyed gaze flat and his face deadpan. Thought I'd earned more than that, but there wasn't even a hint of a smile; the bastard was damned hard to read at the best of times. He was married to a seriously cute helo pilot from the Night Stalkers, but I was careful to not even glance at her when Lieutenant Bruce was around. The man might be an officer, but he was also a Unit operator and just as dangerous as any of us. He also hung tight with Colonel Gibson who was more dangerous than all of us combined.

"Anything cooking on the desk?"...*other than the damned desk in this heat?* I grabbed a water bottle out of the kicker fridge and rubbed it across my forehead—so cold it almost gave me a headache. A mission would make the night much more tolerable, but it all looked pretty damn quiet. The folding table supported a stack of silent comm gear, a couple big screens that were supposed to be for situational displays but streamed movies just fine on pizza-and-no beer nights—dry post on Saudi soil.

"Left you some routine crap," Bill flicked a finger against the paper in the in-basket.

"Thanks so much, asshole." I gave it a friendly tone.

He glanced at me. There were certain looks that they only teach in officer's school and this was one of them.

"Thanks so much, asshole Sir." *Shit!* Still nothing. There was no saluting in the field. It might attract a sniper's bullet targeted at whoever that identified as being in charge. But I was tempted just in case there was a sniper on the hunt tonight, because that would at least change the mood.

The lieutenant tapped the pile again, marking it as my top priority, before heading out into the dark heat.

The small fan perched on the edge of the desk helped a little when I dropped into the folding steel chair. Now instead of slowly baking to death, I was going to be put out of my misery much sooner by the blowtorch of fan-driven hot air.

Comms were silent. I logged into the computer and made sure the command message queue was up on the screen. I popped up a second window that showed the regional queue as well. Nothing but a whole lot of quiet. I could have heard a gecko walking on the metal ceiling a dozen meters above me.

Feet on the desk, I pulled over the in-basket and began flipping through it. Some supply chain crap. New sergeant coming over soon. No sign of my reassignment to somewhere, anywhere else, not that I was expecting one anytime soon but I could always hope. I'd give up my next pay for two damned minutes of Oregon Coast air—just a walk with my lady down the long sand beaches; the wind off the Pacific rolling in cool, wet, and so fresh it was like no one had ever breathed it before.

Dreaming of other places, I had the manila folder from deep in the pile half open before

I froze in place. The chill up my spine had a whole lot more to do with Arctic training than Saudi desert. I almost shouted out *Landmine!* to warn everyone around me—except if I did, only the plane and helicopters were there to hear me. I was sitting alone and holding a viper made out of beige manila—a viper way more dangerous than the flesh-and-blood kind.

"Classified-Secret."

A big red stamp on the cover. Typically illegible authorization signature. An innocuous number on the tab.

Why the hell was a classified document buried in the watch desk in-basket? I wanted to take the damn thing and ram it right up the lieutenant's ass for leaving such a thing out to be found.

Protocol said to lock it up in the secure vault resting under the table, then report it to command and send an armed guard to take the lieutenant into custody. Reality said to lock it up and suggest to his boss that the man get a refresher course in proper handling of classifieds.

Instead, I eased it open.

"Eyes only!"

Viper? Hell. I was holding a damned grenade with no sign of the pin or handle—and three of five seconds gone.

Should have slapped it closed. Should have the fucking lieutenant shot.

Instead I read the damned thing.

2

Mira slipped into the hangar. The way that woman moved was like nothing else I'd ever seen. There weren't all that many Spec Ops women, but she made it look natural... natural and dangerous as hell. We'd quietly shared enough two-week leaves for me to know that both assessments were accurate about her in every way. Dusky skinned enough to pass as a native anywhere in the Middle East, her night ops black hair curled down to her shoulders. Her face was forgettably normal (which was ideal for an operator)—forgettable unless you knew the woman who hid so carefully behind it.

She didn't ask why I called and woke her. Instead, she sat down on another chair and waited.

I turned the folder over in my lap and showed her the front.

A shrug.

I peeled back the front flap enough to reveal the "Eyes Only."

Her gaze shot up and she inspected me carefully. I could see her connecting pieces, putting together the question that I wasn't willing to speak aloud. I wasn't asking the question of my lover. I was a sniper asking a question of my spotter.

A sniper has to move undercover in any environment—hard to do as a single man, much easier with a woman at his side. He also needs a spotter to watch his back and cover the wider view. She excelled at both roles. Whether we were on overwatch protecting door-kicker troops working the street below or out in the weeds, Mira didn't miss a thing. We were one of the top teams operating.

Mira would of course integrate all this into her consideration about the question I had asked by flashing the folder. She knew she could stand up and walk away with no hard feelings, but she also knew I wouldn't have called her lightly.

This time I couldn't read what was going on behind her dark eyes any more than the damn lieutenant's light ones, but she reached out and took the file.

Based on the data in the folder, I began studying city maps and drone overflight images on the dual screens while she read.

3

*"**We're not supposed to** be here, Kurt!"* Only Mira's eyes showed through the narrow slit of the *niqab* headpiece she'd worn as we worked our way across Riyadh looking like any other Arab couple.

"Then leave." It came out harsher than I intended, but I was feeling the pressure too. "Sorry." The "home" we were surveying would have been a mansion in Los Angeles, a damned big one. Here it was called a palace but that didn't make it any smaller.

I could tell by the narrowing of her eyes that Mira was scowling at me, which I ignored just as I had been for the other fifty times she'd said it since last night. Though once she'd read the file there hadn't been any question of not going in together. Something about complaining made her feel like she was in control whenever the situation was spinning out of control, but I knew that about her and usually let it slide.

Didn't matter anyway.

Once we stepped past this point we'd be in it deep and the only way out was going to be even uglier than the way in. In truth, all bets were on a one-way ticket.

We weren't supposed to be here—no one could know. Literally... No. One. That's what the Unit specialized in, but even by our standards this was beyond dark and creepy.

The objective was inside this monstrosity. Four stories with a double-height first. Delta named the sides of a building from front entrance around clockwise by the alphabet for easy reference—front door wall was "A," next wall to the right "B," and so on. Don't know if this place would have fit in the alphabet. Shining white, two big wings, attached garages that would fit twenty cars, bathhouses between the two pools, a clubhouse by the putting greens… The place was absurd. Thankfully, that worked in our favor as the target would never think guards were needed every foot. It was old enough that the cameras and sensors had been installed later, making them both easy to spot and fewer than they should have been.

Mira was right though, this was the last check-in, the last point to turn back.

I flicked a "Move Out" sign, but more as a question. At Mira's nod, we shed our outer robes. From here on, blending in wasn't the issue, being invisible was. Dark camouflage, night-vision goggles, and minimal gear other than our weapons and a lot of extra rounds. We headed in.

They didn't train snipers in The Unit to waste time. Our training was all about achieving results. I wasn't the first operator to have used that as an excuse in marginal conditions and I wasn't about to be the last. Because we delivered, Joint Special Operations Command did a fine job of looking the other way.

When we were rolling up Iraqi terror cells back in the war, the Status of Forces Agreement prohibited US counterterrorism raids without an Iraqi court-issued warrant. To solve this, Spec Ops built courtrooms in every major city in-country and made sure they were manned by US lawyers and a local judge 24/7. Still, the ops in the field sometimes outstripped the speed of the courts. When we had a known terrorist in our sights, the lawyers back-timed the judge's signature and the judge turned a blind eye.

Were mistakes made?

Very few and only very quiet ones.

The Unit wasn't SEAL Team Six. ST6 made noise about their ops—Captain Phillips, bin Laden, Jessica Buchanan; high profile wasn't in our program. With command's and the Iraqi courts' authorization, four thousand Al-Qaeda leaders were removed in the last four years of the Iraq War. It all happened so quietly that local Al-Qaeda required years of inattention by Iraq Security Forces in order to rebuild into any level of viable threat. Noise wasn't the Unit's way. Wasn't really ST6's either, but the newsies had latched onto them so hard they could barely take a shit without hitting the headlines—better them than us.

This op wasn't exactly authorized either.

No warrant had been issued.

No war existed here.

No order had been issued.

Except for what was in that goddamn folder, which probably no longer existed. When I hand-delivered the thing back to Lieutenant Bruce, an "Oh, thanks Master Sergeant," was all I got for my trouble.

That and a headful of crap I wished I never knew.

This was a friendly country, an ally, even the kind that The Unit usually cultivated—a dangerous one.

The Kingdom of Saudi Arabia spent more per capita on their military than any other country. Number One. The Big Kahuna. The KSA spent three times the amount that Singapore, Israel, or even the US did. Five times more than anyone in the next tier down. A higher percentage of their annual GDP than anyone except North Korea and that place was fucked anyway.

Mira and I slid in through the garage: Bentley, Rolls, Lambo, Porsche, not a whole lot of American other than a Humvee and a

Tesla. No Japanese at all. Got to admit that the Lamborghini Countach was a classic that almost stopped me in my tracks—it was a low-slung craft of beauty.

Mira nudged me with the butt of her rifle. "Boys and toys," she whispered but I could hear the laugh in it.

I hadn't felt much like laughing since I'd spent the hours reading that goddamn document before I called Mira.

The KSA was run by one king and seven thousand princes, all blood relatives. Family reunions must be hell. Especially with how these guys got along. Internecine conflict didn't begin to describe it. And when huge bulks of oil fortunes were on the move, it got messy. Defense Ministers took billion dollar bribes from foreign military vendors like it was cotton candy. Lately the Saudis had been going through Ministers of Defense and the Interior so fast it was a wonder anyone was left in the royal family, because sure as shit if you were one of the top thirty, you were related by direct blood to the king and your motives were suspect.

Some of the princes were pro-American,

some anti-. That didn't bother me any and it hadn't bothered Mira when I was giving her the lay of the land. It's not like that was any news to us. Both of our fathers had done the Desert Storm dance, staging in The KSA to clear Saddam Hussein out of Kuwait. They'd both brought back plenty of stories and a gutful of hate.

But I hadn't meant to suck Mira all of the way in. I had just wanted her take on the file's contents. Was I reading too much into that "Eyes Only" report or…apparently not.

Saudi Prince Abdul Malik Hassan was demanding heavy "donations" for feeding the US with prime intel. Turned out that he also was taking prime intel on our movements and selling them back to every bidder.

Twenty-five of my SEAL Team 6 brothers— I only sneer at them to keep them on their toes—were in a Chinook helo that was shot down in Afghanistan in 2011. Deep research pointed to Abdul feeding the intel to Al-Qaeda shooters—no proof. Again when ST6 had been repulsed by Al-Shabaab terrorists in Somalia, Abdul's call had been traced there as well. He had a whole network of brothers, cousins, and sons servicing the intel in both directions—a clusterfuck that involved a dozen princes and twenty more besides. We needed the intelligence reports he gave us, so the CIA had labeled him "Untouchable."

There were other opinions in that damn file. The Saudi Defense Minister, the US Secretary of State, the Head of the Joint Chiefs, a scribble that just might be the President's initials... They all agreed that Abdul had walked way too far over the lines in both directions. But no one wanted to do the deed. No one wanted the CIA to find out they'd done the deed.

And neither Mira nor I gave a shit about any of them.

It was the price of what Abdul took...

I no longer had brothers, not outside the service. No family outside the service.

My brother Stan found heroin, then God, then tried combining the two so that he could go meet God face to face. He never came back to tell me if it worked. Mom had long since walked away and Dad eventually ate his gun. We weren't what you'd call...close.

"Close" is what I found in The Unit, even before I met Mira Stenkowski.

Five years in Special Forces, tromping ass with the 3rd SFG Green Berets, before I could even apply to The Unit. Delta Assessment Phase spent a month proving that nobody loved me—but I already knew that, so it didn't knock me out like so many others. Combined with being tough as hell, I made the five percent cut. And they took me in.

All the way in.

The Unit did that. These weren't fellow soldiers. The guys weren't some inbred clan like Prince Abdul's. These were men, and now the few women, that I'd stand at the tip of the spear for. Give me the first hit. Take me down first. Because that's the only way you're going to get at me and mine.

But Abdul didn't believe in belonging.

4

For three days we watched him.

Mira and I crawled in and watched him. We lived in his house. We smelled the food he ate. We watched him fuck his wives at night from so close we could smell the sex on him afterward. We didn't drink water so that we wouldn't have to pee. We didn't eat so that we wouldn't have to shit.

Mira and I were a US Delta Force sniper team—so invisible that we weren't even there.

But we were and we listened.

Abdul had a rage in him. That part of him I recognized. That part of him I knew down to my bones. Before The Unit, it had twisted inside my guts like a knife every time I thought of my family. I didn't beat or kill, but I knew what drove him.

He got angry at a wife for not being eager to receive him. After he beat her, and used her hard, he stated the fateful "I divorce you" three times—all a guy had to do to end a marriage in this culture. At that moment she lost rights to any of her children and was banished back to her family, never to emerge from the shame again. Mira almost took him down at that point, but I held her back. Abdul wasn't the only reason we were here.

A cousin of his—who had demanded a mere hundred grand for selling the allied bombing patterns over a terrorist-held city when he should have earned half a million— was dismissed, without the grace-saving of "based on his request" in the announcement of his departure. His career, his life in Saudi politics was finished. Mira and I laid a bet that his fortunes would be gone in twenty-four hours and his family in forty-eight. *End it now, Dude.*

And still we waited in thirsty silence.

We were the hum in an air-conditioning vent, a shadow behind a palm tree, a breath on the wind. We sucked on pebbles to draw precious saliva to soothe aching throats.

Three long days we waited and watched. On the long watches I wondered if the goddamn lieutenant had reported us AWOL—away without leave—or if he'd left a simple "on assignment" on our registers. We were past that now. Even the ache didn't matter, only the mission.

The self-assigned mission.

Night four.

Abdul's private war council had finally been called.

Out in the great courtyard of his home, an evening of food and debauchery on a grand scale convened. His war council of thirty of his closest and most trusted—brothers, cousins, sons. All of his sons.

"Go, Mira. Go now. While you can." I was assembling my McMillan sniper rifle.

"That boat sailed the minute we stepped off the reservation, Kurt." She began lining up magazines for me. Five rounds per mag of .50 BMG sniper-grade ammo; four to a pound and as long as the five dollar bill each one cost. We'd scouted the ideal spot, found it in the bastard's bedroom. A monstrous bed, satin sheets the size of pool covers, red Persian rugs on white marble floors, gold fixtures in a bathroom big enough to park a couple Humvees in. Wealth dripped out of the faucets and shone from the crystal chandeliers. I'd never seen anything like it and frankly never wanted to again. It was cold in this blazingly hot country. More frigid and heartless than a winter storm blowing in off the north Pacific.

Mira had quietly spoken with the four current wives—apparently none of them were very fond of their husband-prince and the dismissed wife had been a favorite in their circle. For their own safety in deniability afterward, Mira had tied them up in the bathroom. Then we'd barricaded ourselves in.

The only opening was the French doors that swung out into the night. An ornate dresser of inlaid English rosewood turned into a shooting stand placed well inside the room. With the flash suppressor and an extra foot of silencer, I'd attract little attention. Only a perfect shot from the courtyard could find me, though we both expected one eventually would.

Mira's family had been little better than mine. Just like me, her brothers and now the occasional sister, were in the Special Operations community. We both knew what was coming for us and, without a word, we were both willing to pay the price if it came to that.

Abdul's war council spread out in the marble-paved courtyard below me—acres of the stuff. Out in the exact center stood a circle of tables covered with pristine white cloths and laden with an unimaginable bounty. Buckets of iced caviar, great slabs of pâté, whole sides of beef that could feed hundreds, all served by lightly clad women who had clearly been paid to not complain no matter what was done to them.

The range was so close that I couldn't miss.

The Canadian Tac-50 was twenty-six pounds and six-feet of the baddest rifle in the business. Two of the three longest sniper shots ever confirmed as kills had flown out of Tac-50 barrels—each over two thousand yards and I didn't have a single shot here over two hundred. I'd selected the beast just in case I had needed the long shot. Instead I had easy targets and massive rounds to punch with.

I dialed back my Schmidt-Bender scope all the way to compensate for the thousand-yard zeroing I kept the rifle set for. My bullets were going to drop less than two inches before impact at this range.

We'd all been scrubbed. There was no serial number on either scope or weapon. The only ID Mira and I carried was phony as hell and identified us as mercenaries gone hunting— traceably hired by the remains of a cell of terrorists Abdul had fucked over in Pakistan. Even if we got out clean, we'd "drop" those IDs somewhere that they'd be discovered.

US intel services wanted him in place. US and Saudi military—and any grunt with even half a brain—wanted him gone no matter what the CIA said. He was about to be erased.

I was committing an act of war. Killing thirty of the King of Saudi Arabia's immediate relatives couldn't be shrugged off. One or two might be overlooked, but Abdul had built his network too well and just cutting the head off the serpent wouldn't be enough.

Worst case scenario? There would be two

dead mercs who would never be identified, except by Combat Applications Group Lieutenant Bruce—who'd known exactly what he was doing when he left that "Eyes Only" report for a sniper and his spotter, both with no families outside The Unit.

I snapped in the first magazine with a gentle click and worked the bolt to load the first round so softly that it wouldn't have disturbed a cricket.

Two hundred yards away, I stared straight into Prince Abdul Malik Hassan's face through my scope. His head filled my view. It was thrown back in a laugh and it would have been so easy to feed a round to him, right down his throat.

You always heard when an ST6 SEAL died in action. His brothers saw to that, but that wasn't our way. When my best friend went down in Yemen, his family never knew how it happened. But I knew, now that I'd read the file—they traced it to Abdul giving away our plans. When Mira's bunkmate lost both arms and her eyesight in the Ukraine, Abdul might as well have pulled the trigger.

"Not yet, Abdul," I whispered down the long length of my sweet rifle.

I shifted my aim.

Not yet.

First you need to watch your family die.

5

The Unit doesn't believe in suicide missions. Delta's mission is to deliver results. I'd arrived in this place knowing the odds. I care about my life and Mira's, maybe more than anyone because an operator goes in knowing the risks—I take them every day. It would take so little to erase everything except someone's memory of me. A stray round, a single mistake.

Training taught me that, but it might not have been enough. I wanted Abdul so badly that I would have seen it through even if there had been no chance of escape.

It was Mira who had taught me that there

was more, so much more. We'd slowly discovered it together, in each other. Two people learning that there was family beyond our brothers and sisters of war. Until we ultimately found true family in each other. There was nothing we wouldn't do for one another.

Nothing.

We began.

It was messy, but it was fast. After three days lying in wait, it was no more than an eyeblink. One heartbeat between shots and three to reload. Just thirty seconds to clear the courtyard of every target—but one.

Then Abdul went down, hard. He went down screaming in panic and running away from the circle of the dead: his murdering council of friends and relatives. For him I used three full magazines, fifteen rounds, all blasted from the big Tac-50 to take him apart one piece at a time.

Toward the end I was peripherally aware of other gunfire—silenced rounds on a different beat—but that wasn't my focus. That's why I had a spotter and if she wasn't good enough, we were both done.

She was.

The silence echoed through the courtyard, Abdul's final scream no more than a memory in the vast marble plaza. Our gunfire had been quiet pops never heard beyond the French doors. Beside many of the dead lay drawn weapons, but lacking a target, no shot was fired.

Mira and I eased back through the streets of Riyadh in the soft cool breath of the pre-dawn desert. She walked two steps behind me, as a *niqab*-clad woman should follow her man: respectful, hidden. Her rifle, like mine, still warm from use, they too now lay hidden beneath the long folds of her robe. Only her eyes showed.

But in my mind's eye she moved beside me, her dark hair floating free in the ocean's winds as we held hands and walked together down the beach in a soft, cool Oregon rain— her dark eyes bright with the joy of being alive.

About the Author

M. L. Buchman has over 40 novels in print. His military romantic suspense books have been named Barnes & Noble and NPR "Top 5 of the year" and *Booklist* "Top 10 of the Year." He has been nominated for the Reviewer's Choice Award for "Top 10 Romantic Suspense of 2014" by *RT Book Reviews*. In addition to romance, he also writes thrillers, fantasy, and science fiction.

In among his career as a corporate project manager he has: rebuilt and single-handed a fifty-foot sailboat, both flown and jumped out of airplanes, designed and built two houses, and bicycled solo around the world.

He is now making his living as a full-time writer on the Oregon Coast with his beloved wife. He is constantly amazed at what you can do with a degree in Geophysics. You may keep up with his writing by subscribing to his newsletter at www.mlbuchman.com.

Target Engaged (excerpt)
-a Delta Force novel-

Carla Anderson rolled up to the looming, storm-fence gate on her brother's midnight-blue Kawasaki Ninja 1000 motorcycle. The pounding of the engine against her sore butt emphasized every mile from Fort Carson in Pueblo, Colorado, home of the 4th Infantry and hopefully never again the home of

Sergeant Carla Anderson. The bike was all she had left of Clay, other than a folded flag, and she was here to honor that.

If this was the correct "here."

A small guard post stood by the gate into a broad, dusty compound. It looked deserted and she didn't see even a camera.

This *was* Fort Bragg, North Carolina. She knew that much. Two hundred and fifty square miles of military installation, not counting the addition of the neighboring Pope Army Airfield.

She'd gotten her Airborne parachute training here and had never even known what was hidden in this remote corner. Bragg was exactly the sort of place where a tiny, elite unit of the U.S. military could disappear—in plain sight.

This back corner of the home of the 82nd Airborne was harder to find than it looked. What she could see of the compound through the fence definitely ranked "worst on base."

The setup was totally whacked.

Standing outside the fence at the guard post she could see a large, squat building across the compound. The gray concrete building was incongruously cheerful with bright pink roses along the front walkway—the only landscaping visible anywhere. More recent buildings—in better condition only because they were newer—ranged off to the right. She could breach the old fence in a dozen different places just in the hundred-yard span she could see before it disappeared into a clump of scrub and low trees drooping in the June heat.

Wholly indefensible.

There was no way that this could be the headquarters of the top combat unit in any country's military.

Unless this really was their home, in which case the indefensible fence—inde-fence-ible?— was a complete sham designed to fool a sucker. She'd stick with the main gate.

She peeled off her helmet and scrubbed at her long brown hair to get some air back into her scalp. Guys always went gaga over her hair, which was a useful distraction at times. She always wore it as long as her successive commanders allowed. Pushing the limits was one of her personal life policies.

She couldn't help herself. When there was a limit, Carla always had to see just how far it could be nudged. Surprisingly far was usually the answer. Her hair had been at earlobe length in Basic. By the time she joined her first forward combat team, it brushed her jaw. Now it was down on her shoulders. It was actually something of a pain in the ass at this length— another couple inches before it could reliably ponytail—but she did like having the longest hair in the entire unit.

Carla called out a loud "Hello!" at the empty compound shimmering in the heat haze.

No response.

Using her boot in case the tall chain-link fence was electrified, she gave it a hard shake, making it rattle loudly in the dead air. Not even any birdsong in the oppressive midday heat.

A rangy man in his late forties or early fifties, his hair half gone to gray, wandered around from behind a small shack as if he just happened to be there by chance. He was dressed like any off-duty soldier: worn khaki pants, a black T-shirt, and scuffed Army boots. He slouched to a stop and tipped his head to study her from behind his Ray-Bans. He needed a haircut and a shave. This was not a soldier out to make a good first impression.

"Don't y'all get hot in that gear?" He nodded

to indicate her riding leathers without raking his eyes down her frame, which was unusual and appreciated.

"Only on warm days," she answered him. It was June in North Carolina. The temperature had crossed ninety hours ago and the air was humid enough to swim in, but complaining never got you anywhere.

"What do you need?"

So much for the pleasantries. "Looking for Delta."

"Never heard of it," the man replied with a negligent shrug. But something about how he did it told her she was in the right place.

"Combat Applications Group?" Delta Force had many names, and they certainly lived to "apply combat" to a situation. No one on the planet did it better.

His next shrug was eloquent.

Delta Lesson One: *Folks on the inside of the wire didn't call it Delta Force. It was CAG or "The Unit."* She got it. Check. Still easier to think of it as Delta though.

She pulled out her orders and held them up. "Received a set of these. Says to show up here today."

"Let me see that."

"Let me through the gate and you can look at it as long as you want."

"Sass!" He made it an accusation.

"Nope. I just don't want them getting damaged or lost maybe by accident." She offered her blandest smile with that.

"They're that important to you, girlie?"

"Yep!"

He cracked what might have been the start of a grin, but it didn't get far on that grim face. Then he opened the gate and she idled the bike forward, scuffing her boots through the dust.

From this side she could see that the chain link was wholly intact. There was a five-meter swath of scorched earth inside the fence line. Through the heat haze, she could see both infrared and laser spy eyes down the length of the wire. And that was only the defenses she could see. So...a very *not* inde-fence-ible fence. Absolutely the right place.

When she went to hold out the orders, he waved them aside.

"Don't you want to see them?" This had to be the right place. She was the first woman in history to walk through The Unit's gates by order. A part of her wanted the man to acknowledge that. Any man. A Marine Corps marching band wouldn't have been out of order.

She wanted to stand again as she had on that very first day, raising her right hand. "I, Carla Anderson, do solemnly swear that I will support and defend the Constitution…"

She shoved that aside. The only man's acknowledgment she'd ever cared about was her big brother's, and he was gone.

The man just turned away and spoke to her over his shoulder as he closed the gate behind her bike. "Go ahead and check in. You're one of the last to arrive. We start in a couple hours"—as if it were a blasted dinner party. "And I already saw those orders when I signed them. Now put them away before someone else sees them and thinks you're still a soldier." He walked away.

She watched the man's retreating back. *He'd* signed her orders?

That was the notoriously hard-ass Colonel Charlie Brighton?

What the hell was the leader of the U.S. Army's Tier One asset doing manning the gate? Duh…assessing new applicants.

This place *was* whacked. Totally!

There were only three Tier One assets in the entire U.S. military. There was Navy's Special Warfare Development Group, DEVGRU, that the public thought was called SEAL Team Six—although it hadn't been named that for thirty years now. There was the Air Force's 24th STS—which pretty much no one on the outside had ever heard of. And there was the 1st Special Forces Operational Detachment—Delta—whose very existence was still denied by the Pentagon despite four decades of operations, several books, and a couple of seriously off-the-mark movies that were still fun to watch because Chuck Norris kicked ass even under the stupidest of circumstances.

Total Tier One women across all three teams? Zero.

About to be? One. Staff Sergeant First Class Carla Anderson.

Where did she need to go to check in? There was no signage. No drill sergeant hovering. No—

Delta Lesson Number Two: *You aren't in the Army anymore, sister.*

No longer a soldier, as the Colonel had

said, at least not while on The Unit's side of the fence. On this side they weren't regular Army; they were "other."

If that meant she had to take care of herself, well, that was a lesson she'd learned long ago. Against stereotype, her well-bred, East Coast white-guy dad was the drunk. Her dirt-poor half Tennessee Cherokee, half Colorado settler mom, who'd passed her dusky skin and dark hair on to her daughter, had been a sober and serious woman. She'd also been a casualty of an Afghanistan dust-bowl IED while serving in the National Guard. Carla's big brother Clay now lay beside Mom in Arlington National Cemetery. Dead from a training accident. Except your average training accident didn't include a posthumous rank bump, a medal, and coming home in a sealed box reportedly with no face.

Clay had flown helicopters in the Army's 160th SOAR with the famous Majors Beale and Henderson. Well, famous in the world of people who'd flown with the Special Operations Aviation Regiment, or their little sisters who'd begged for stories of them whenever big brothers were home on leave. Otherwise totally invisible.

Clay had clearly died on a black op that she'd never be told a word of, so she didn't bother asking. Which was okay. He knew the risks, just as Mom had. Just as she herself had when she'd signed up the day of Clay's funeral, four years ago. She'd been on the front lines ever since and so far lived to tell about it.

Carla popped Clay's Ninja—which is how she still thought of it, even after riding it for four years—back into first and rolled it slowly up to the building with the pink roses. As good a place to start as any.

***

"Hey, check out this shit!"

Sergeant First Class Kyle Reeves looked out the window of the mess hall at the guy's call. Sergeant Ralph last-name-already-forgotten was 75th Rangers and too damn proud of it.

Though…damn! Ralphie was onto something.

Kyle would definitely check out *this shit*.

Babe on a hot bike, looking like she knew how to handle it.

Through the window, he inspected her lean length as she clambered off the machine.

Army boots. So call her five-eight, a hundred and thirty, and every part that wasn't amazing curves looked like serious muscle. Hair the color of lush, dark caramel brushed her shoulders but moved like the finest silk, her skin permanently the color of the darkest tan. Women in magazines didn't look that hot. Those women always looked anorexic to him anyway, even the pinup babes displayed on Hesco barriers at forward operating bases up in the Hindu Kush where he'd done too much of the last couple years.

This woman didn't look like that for a second. She looked powerful. And dangerous.

Her tight leathers revealed muscles made of pure soldier.

Ralph Something moseyed out of the mess-hall building where the hundred selectees were hanging out to await the start of the next testing class at sundown.

Well, Kyle sure wasn't going to pass up the opportunity for a closer look. Though seeing Ralph's attitude, Kyle hung back a bit so that he wouldn't be too closely associated with the dickhead.

Ralph had been spoiling for a fight ever

since he'd found out he was one of the least experienced guys to show up for Delta selection. He was from the 75th Ranger Regiment, but his deployments hadn't seen much action. Each of his attempts to brag for status had gotten him absolutely nowhere.

Most of the guys here were 75th Rangers, 82nd Airborne, or Green Beret Special Forces like himself. And most had seen a shitload of action because that was the nature of the world at the moment. There were a couple SEALs who hadn't made SEAL Team Six and probably weren't going to make Delta, a dude from the Secret Service Hostage Rescue Team who wasn't going to last a day no matter how good a shot he was, and two guys who were regular Army.

The question of the moment though, who was she?

Her biking leathers were high-end, sewn in a jagged lightning-bolt pattern of yellow on smoke gray. It made her look like she was racing at full tilt while standing still. He imagined her hunched over her midnight-blue machine and hustling down the road at her Ninja's top speed—which was north of 150.

He definitely had to see that one day.

Kyle blessed the inspiration on his last leave that had made him walk past the small Toyota pickup that had looked so practical and buy the wildfire-red Ducati Multistrada 1200 instead. Pity his bike was parked around the back of the barracks at the moment. Maybe they could do a little bonding over their rides. Her machine looked absolutely cherry.

Much like its rider.

Ralph walked right up to her with all his arrogant and stupid hanging out for everyone to see. The other soldiers began filtering outside to watch the show.

"Well, girlie, looks like you pulled into the wrong spot. This here is Delta territory."

Kyle thought about stopping Ralph, thought that someone should give the guy a good beating, but Dad had taught him control. He would take Ralph down if he got aggressive, but he really didn't want to be associated with the jerk, even by grabbing him back.

The woman turned to face them, then unzipped the front of her jacket in one of those long, slow movie moves. The sunlight shimmered across her hair as she gave it an "unthinking" toss. Wraparound dark glasses hid her eyes, adding to the mystery.

He could see what there was of Ralph's brain imploding from lack of blood. He felt the effect himself despite standing a half-dozen paces farther back.

She wasn't hot; she sizzled. Her parting leathers revealed an Army green T-shirt and proof that the very nice contours suggested by her outer gear were completely genuine. Her curves weren't big—she had a lean build—but they were as pure woman as her shoulders and legs were pure soldier.

"There's a man who called me 'girlie' earlier." Her voice was smooth and seductive, not low and throaty, but rich and filled with nuance.

She sounded like one of those people who could hypnotize a Cobra, either the snake or the attack helicopter.

"He's a bird colonel. He can call me that if he wants. You aren't nothing but meat walking on sacred ground and wishing he belonged."

Kyle nodded to himself. The "girlie" got it in one.

"*You*"—she jabbed a finger into Sergeant

Ralph Something's chest—"do not get 'girlie' privileges. *We* clear?"

"Oh, sweetheart, I can think of plenty of privileges that you'll want to be giving to—" His hand only made it halfway to stroking her hair.

If Kyle hadn't been Green Beret trained, he wouldn't have seen it because she moved so fast and clean.

"—*me!*" Ralph's voice shot upward on a sharp squeak.

The woman had Ralph's pinkie bent to the edge of dislocation and, before the man could react, had leveraged it behind his back and upward until old Ralph Something was perched on his toes trying to ease the pressure. With her free hand, she shoved against the middle of his back to send him stumbling out of control into the concrete wall of the mess hall with a loud *clonk* when his head hit.

Minimum force, maximum result. The Unit's way.

She eased off on his finger and old Ralph dropped to the dirt like a sack of potatoes. He didn't move much.

"Oops." She turned to face the crowd that had gathered.

She didn't even have to say, "Anyone else?" Her look said plenty.

Kyle began to applaud. He wasn't the only one, but he was in the minority. Most of the guys were doing a wait and see.

A couple looked pissed.

Everyone knew that the Marines' combat training had graduated a few women, but that was just jarheads on the ground.

This was Delta. The Unit was Tier One. A Special Mission Unit. They were supposed to be the one true bastion of male dominance. No one had warned them that a woman was coming in.

Just one woman, Kyle thought. The first one. How exceptional did that make her? Pretty damn was his guess. Even if she didn't last the first day, still pretty damn. And damn pretty. He'd bet on dark eyes behind her wraparound shades. She didn't take them off, so it was a bet he'd have to settle later on.

A couple corpsmen came over and carted Ralph Something away even though he was already sitting up—just dazed with a bloody cut on his forehead.

The Deltas who'd come out to watch the

show from a few buildings down didn't say a word before going back to whatever they'd been doing.

Kyle made a bet with himself that Ralph Something wouldn't be showing up at sundown's first roll call. They'd just lost the first one of the class and the selection process hadn't even begun. Or maybe it just had.

"Where's check-in?" Her voice really was as lush as her hair, and it took Kyle a moment to focus on the actual words.

He pointed at the next building over and received a nod of thanks.

That made watching her walk away in those tight leathers strictly a bonus.

Available at fine retailers everywhere.

Other works by M.L. Buchman

<u>Delta Force</u>
Target Engaged

<u>Firehawks</u>
Pure Heat
Wildfire at Dawn
Full Blaze
Wildfire at Larch Creek
Wildfire on the Skagit
Hot Point

<u>The Night Stalkers</u>
The Night Is Mine
I Own the Dawn
Daniel's Christmas
Wait Until Dark
Frank's Independence Day
Peter's Christmas
Take Over at Midnight
Light Up the Night
Bring On the Dusk
Target of the Heart
Target Lock on Love
Christmas at Peleliu Cove
Zachary's Christmas

<u>Angelo's Hearth</u>
Where Dreams are Born
Where Dreams Reside
Maria's Christmas Table
Where Dreams Unfold
Where Dreams Are Written

<u>Dieties Anonymous</u>
Cookbook from Hell: Reheated
Saviors 101

<u>Thrillers</u>
Swap Out!
One Chef!
Two Chef!

<u>SF/F Titles</u>
Nara
Monk's Maze

newsletter signup at:
www.mlbuchman.com

Made in the USA
Lexington, KY
21 March 2016